D1265979

KIDDING AROUND

by Claire Griffin
illustrated by Jane Chambless Wright

Instructional Fair • TS Denison • Grand Rapids, MI

A Note to Parents and Teachers

The *Rollicking Rhymes* series of stories is written especially for pre-readers and beginning readers. The rhymes are based on a limited number of word families, so that readers can recognize the ending sounds of the words and develop fluency faster. Many rhymes also feature predictable repetitions of key words and phrases to help your child learn other words more quickly as well. The humor and whimsical illustrations found throughout the *Rollicking Rhymes* series help engage and keep the attention of new readers. In *Kidding Around*, children will recognize familiar family situations, and they will connect with the funny way these events are presented.

Library of Congress Cataloging-in-Publication Data

Griffin, Claire Janosik, 1950-
    Kidding around / by Claire Griffin ; illustrated by Jane Chambless Wright.
      p. cm. -- (Rollicking rhymes)
    Summary: Two stories in rhyme about a girl who wants to get rid of her baby brother and children who have to behave at a luncheon.
    ISBN 1-56822-978-X (hardcover)
    1. Children's stories, American. [1. Babies--Fiction. 2. Brothers and sisters--Fiction. 3. Behavior--Fiction. 4. Short stories. 5. Stories in rhyme.] I. Wright, Jane Chambless, ill. II. Title. III. Series.

PZ8.3.G868 Ki 2000
[E]--dc21

00-022241

Credits

Author: Claire Griffin
Cover and Inside Illustrations: Jane Chambless Wright
Creative Director: Annette Hollister-Papp
Project Director/Editor: Kathryn Wheeler
Editors: Alyson Kieda, Linda Triemstra
Cover Design: Peggy Jackson
Page Design: Ruth Ostrowski-DeKorne

ISBN: 1-56822-978-X
Kidding Around
Copyright © 2000 by Instructional Fair • TS Denison
A Division of Instructional Fair Group, Inc.
A Tribune Education Company
3195 Wilson Drive NW
Grand Rapids, Michigan 49544

All rights reserved. No part of this publication may be reproduced, stored in a retrieval system, or transmitted, in any form or by any means, electronic, mechanical, photocopying, recording, or otherwise, without the prior written permission of the publisher.

For information regarding permission write to:
Instructional Fair • TS Denison, P.O. Box 1650, Grand Rapids, MI 49501.

Printed in Singapore

New Brother

I don't know why I asked for a brother.

"Let's send him away!" I tell my mother.

"Where could we send him?" she wants to know.

"Off to the circus! He can be in the show!
The seals could balance him just like a ball,
And toss him around, since he is so small!

4

Or he could go on a trip down the Nile.
He could ride on the back of a crocodile!

A hippo might like him for a pet.
I think that's my best idea yet!

7

Or he could go up in a hot-air balloon.
He could be the first baby to land on the moon!

GREEN CHEESE OR BUST!

9

He might even decide to travel to Mars
Or go even farther—on past the stars.

There are so many places that he could go . . .
But if he wants to come here, Mom, we can just tell him NO!"

Lunch with Grandma

Grandma's taking us out to eat.

Mom says that this will be a treat.

But that's not how it seems to me.

How much fun can it really be?

All of my cousins will be there,
But we can't show our underwear.
No tossing rolls or throwing peas.
We'll just sit looking at our knees.

No sticking straws in ears and noses
Or standing up in silly poses.

16

No frogs dropped down Aunt Annie's back
To watch her fake a heart attack.

17

No rubber snakes or any pranks.

18

Just "Sit still," "Quiet," "Say please and thanks."

This lunch is going to be so boring,
I bet we all just end up snoring!

20